FIRESTORMERS

Firestormers is published by
Stone Arch Books,
a Capstone imprint
1710 Roe Crest Drive
North Mankato, Minnesota 56003
www.mycapstone.com

Cataloging-in-Publication Data is available on the
Library of Congress website.
ISBN: 978-1-4965-3306-7 (library binding)
ISBN: 978-1-4965-3310-4 (eBook)

Summary:
As a historic wildfire bears down on a desolate,
close-knit community, the FIRESTORMERS, the world's
newest, most elite wildfire fighting crew, prepare to
battle the blaze. Unfortunately, community members
would rather die than leave their homes and belongings
behind. As tornadoes of fire approach, Firestormer Amalia
Rendon must convince citizens to evacuate before their
community and everything in it becomes a smoldering
bone yard.

Printed and bound in Canada.
009638F16

FIRESTORMERS
BONE YARD

written by CARL BOWEN
cover illustration by MARC LEE

STONE ARCH BOOKS
a capstone imprint

CONTENTS

FIRESTORMERS

Elite Firefighting Crew

As the climate changes and the population grows, wildland fires increase in number, size, and severity. Only an elite group of men and women are equipped to take on these immense infernos. Like the toughest military units, they have the courage, the heart, and the technology to stand on the front lines against hundred-foot walls of 2,000-degree flames. They are the FIRESTORMERS.

DENALI NATIONAL PARK

Established:

February 26, 1917

Coordinates:

63°20'0" N

150°30'0" W

Location:

Alaska, USA

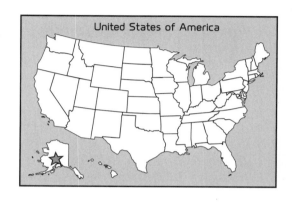

United States of America

Size:

4,740,911 acres (7,407.673 square miles)

Elevation Range:

200–20,320 feet above sea level

Ecology:

Located in the Alaskan interior, between Anchorage and Fairbanks, Denali National Park and Preserve is the most distinct of the state's seven national parks. Although the tallest mountain in North America, Denali (formerly Mount McKinley) towers above the park, many rare and majestic species thrive at its foothills, including grizzly bears, eagles, moose, wolves, and mosses and lichens.

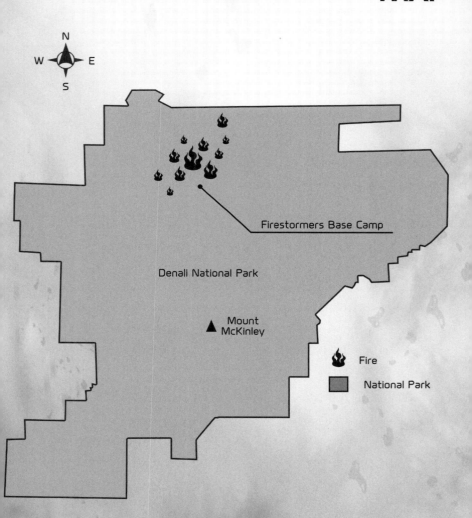

Firestormers Base Camp

Denali National Park

▲ Mount
McKinley

👹 Fire

National Park

CHAPTER ONE

With a huff, Sergeant Amalia Rendon hoisted a roaring twenty-pound chain saw over her head.

"You saw like a girl!" a fellow Firestormer called out.

"Dang straight I do!" she hollered back, letting out a laugh.

Behind her, a seventy-foot black spruce slowly tipped and — WHAM! — came down with a thunderous crash.

Her four-person crew cheered.

Well begun is half done, Rendon thought.

Of course, she knew that this fire was nowhere near half over.

As the felled pine settled on its side, Sergeant Rendon nodded to Corey Edwards, her crew's ranger, and said, "One down . . ."

" . . . and about a million to go," Edwards responded. He grinned and gave her a quick salute and then headed off into the woods.

Sergeant Rendon nodded after him and set her shoulders. *Time to work.*

* * *

Sergeant Rendon was the boss of a four-hand crew of elite wildland firefighters. They belonged to a twenty-five-person strike team consisting of Hotshots and smokejumpers from all over the western United States that had been assembled as part of a recent U.S. Forest Service initiative.

The Forest Service — an agency within the U.S. Department of Agriculture — was responsible for taking care of millions of acres of national forests and grasslands, and one of the greatest dangers to such lands was wildfire.

The current threat: a twenty-thousand-acre wilderness area just outside Denali National Park in Alaska.

Alaska, it turned out, was in serious jeopardy from uncontrolled wildfires. Record numbers of record-setting blazes had all but overwhelmed the state's local fire services. With more wildland than any other state, Alaska had seen more wildfires in recent years than the rest of the lower forty-eight states combined.

Alaska's wildfire problem was so severe, in fact, that the original pitch for the Firestormers program under the previous presidential administration had been as a smaller corps of command staff and strike teams that operated solely in Alaska, aka the "Last Frontier."

The amount of wildfire Alaska endured in a given year would have been dire for any other state. However, Alaska was so vast and its population so sparse that not every fire was an equally urgent emergency. Those that burned in wildlands closest to major cities such as Fairbanks or Anchorage or Juneau were given greater priority.

For those fires, Alaska dedicated the best and brightest from its local fire services. The state also coordinated the efforts of volunteers from fire services in the lower forty-eight and from across the border in Canada. Operating primarily out of Fort Wainwright, Alaska's foremost Incident Command staff put its most trusted firefighters on those blazes that posed the most immediate risk to life and property.

As for the other, lower-priority fires, they

got the attention that could be spared. It wasn't that Alaskan authorities didn't take them seriously, exactly, they just put the needs of their citizens and their economy ahead of those of their wildlands. What's more, the current local leadership was a powerfully, fiercely independent lot — almost to a fault. They weren't too proud to accept what help was offered, but they strongly believed that Alaska's problems were primarily Alaska's to deal with.

They accepted aid and equipment from the Forest Service, but they put that aid toward enhancing their own local efforts. None of them were of a mind to simply turn over command of fire-suppression efforts to federal outsiders. They knew those outsiders would just pack up and leave as soon as the immediate danger appeared to be over.

The fire to which the Firestormers had

been deployed was not the one blowing black smoke all over Fairbanks or the monster tearing its way toward Anchorage. This inferno burned far from civilization.

To say this fire was hardly important in the grand scheme of things would've been an understatement. In fact, if the blaze were burning in any other state, it would have been left to burn itself out on its own as part of the wildland's natural fire cycle.

Alaska, however, couldn't simply let so many fires burn at once across its northern backyards. Over vast swathes of Alaskan wildland, a thick layer of moss, lichen, and other organic materials coats the forest floor beneath the regular undergrowth. This layer, called "duff," has enough organic material in it to smolder and burn even when it's otherwise too damp out for a wildfire to gain much traction. It goes right on burning, keeping the wildfire alive. But the real problem begins when the duff burns away at last, exposing what lies beneath.

Below the rich living organic material of the Last Frontier's wildlands is the hard frozen layer called permafrost. Under normal circumstances, permafrost does not melt. The duff and its overgrowth keeps the permafrost insulated, locked up tight below the surface. When the duff burns, however, it exposes that permafrost and either begins thawing it directly or exposes it to the warming temperatures that will thaw it out in time. The permafrost's frozen rigidity is what gives much of the Alaskan wildland its structure. As it melts, it deforms the land above it, with disastrous consequences.

And so the Forest Service had deployed its Firestormers temporarily to Alaska as part of a long-term effort to slow the rate of permafrost melt.

Rather than thrusting themselves into higher-priority fire suppression efforts where they were not wanted, they were playing their part in the long game. It was a noble and lofty goal, which took some of the sting out of being shut out of the high-stakes action going on farther south, closer to civilization.

***

Less than an hour after splitting off from Lieutenant Jason Garrett and his other crews, Amalia Rendon's crew had made significant progress on their fire line. It wasn't surprising, really. Amalia Rendon was one of the best and brightest among the elite of the elite.

For her, as with other Firestormers, fighting a wildland fire was relatively uncomplicated. Not easy, just uncomplicated.

Sergeant Rendon and her crew scoured the terrain for natural firebreaks, such as canyons, rivers, stony fields, or even highways. From those points, they cut fire lines through the wildland as tightly around the fire as possible. That meant taking down trees and slicing them into manageable logs with chain saws. That meant chopping down saplings and undergrowth with axes and breaking up the ground with picks.

It wasn't the sort of job one could like, exactly — it was too exhausting and nasty for that — but it afforded those who could handle it a unique and universal respect. Sergeant Rendon certainly appreciated that aspect of the work.

That said, there were some days she wished saving the world didn't require quite so much backbreaking drudgery. And the work itself, while physically draining, did allow for a kind of meditative peacefulness once you got into the rhythm of it. The rhythm didn't make the work easier, but it made it easier to deal with.

Sergeant Rendon sought that rhythm as the long, hard fight on the fire line began. She let her thoughts roll backward over the events that had brought her to where she was today.

As her chain saw tucked into the fallen black spruce at her feet and the chips and dust flew, her mind worked its way back to the day she'd gotten the job. She thought she'd known what to expect then, but life had found a way — as it will — to surprise her.

CHAPTER TWO

Amalia Rendon hadn't had much occasion to head back into Albuquerque, New Mexico, since becoming a firefighter. As she fought traffic and searched for a parking space, she remembered why. Making her way from the car to the hotel where her interview was to take place, she was glad she'd decided against wearing the high heels that her previous job had required. She didn't think the occasion called for her beat-up old logging boots, but she also didn't want to skew too fancy either.

Thus, her sensible Mary Janes.

Checking her watch, Rendon crossed the hotel lobby to the concierge desk to find out how to reach the business center. The young man behind the desk looked her up and down and then eagerly told her what she wanted to know. She politely declined his offer to physically walk her there himself.

Attached to the business center was a suite of offices. Chief Anna MacElreath, a veteran fire chief and newly appointed head of the Firestormers squad, had reserved one for the interview. MacElreath was traveling across much of the North- and Southwest to conduct the interviews because the government hadn't yet designated a headquarters for the program's staff. That, and she was also touring western hotspots to survey how local fire services conducted themselves on the job.

A willingness to learn from the locals certainly seemed like a positive quality in a federal administrator. The fact that she'd also been the nation's first female smokejumper was another mark in her favor.

When she found the right room, Rendon straightened her interview jacket, brushed a sprig of lint off her pants leg, and knocked on the door.

"Come on in," a voice drawled from within. Rendon remembered when she heard it that MacElreath's online bio said she'd lived most of her life in Atlanta, Georgia.

Coming in, Rendon found the chief sitting behind a cheap desk with a dime-a-dozen pastoral landscape print hanging on the wall behind it. Chief MacElreath was taller than expected, and Rendon wondered if she had played college basketball like herself.

The chief wore a long-sleeved, button-up shirt and khaki pants. A little less formal than Rendon's own outfit, but she was right not to have worn jeans and boots like she would've preferred.

"Welcome, Ms. Rendon," the chief said. "Nice suit."

Rendon smiled.

"Please, sit." Chief MacElreath shuffled some papers on her desk and then sat as well. "So I've been going over your work history, Amalia. Says here you started out doing weather for a local station after college."

Amalia cocked an eyebrow. "I think what it says is that I was the station's meteorologist. That was my major at UCLA. Well, one of them. That and journalism."

Chief MacElreath smiled at that. "Did you like it? Doing the weather on TV, I mean."

"It had its moments," Rendon replied. "It was just a job, though. Something to pay the bills."

"Says here you did some reporting as well."

"I did," Rendon said.

"Sounds like fun, being on TV. Why'd you want to give that up?"

"Well, I found something a little more worthwhile," Rendon said, trying not to let her irritation show. She'd expected at least one question relevant to her firefighting experience to have come up by now. Seeing as that wasn't the case, she decided to try to steer things back in the right direction herself.

"To be honest, I didn't like playing the 'weather girl' role the station wanted me to play, so I asked if I could put some field pieces together and do some real reporting. The station sent me out on a few fluff pieces as long as I promised to keep doing the weather."

"What sort of fluff pieces?" asked Chief MacElreath.

Rendon shook her head. "County fairs, store openings, movie shoots . . . That sort of thing. Nothing with substance. I complained for about a year, trying to get a story worth doing. Finally, they gave me something to shut me up. The station assigned me a series of stories with the Black Stand Hotshots out in Taos. I hung out with their crew for a couple of weeks, interviewing them, seeing how they train, and what they do on the job. I'd never even heard of Hotshotting before then. But by the time I was done, I realized they were doing a whole lot more good out there than I was ever going to do in front of a green screen."

"I'm glad to hear that you think that way," MacElreath observed. Rendon took a deep, calming breath rather than say the first thing that came to mind. "But, as far as that story you talked about goes, it didn't turn up in any of my research on you."

"Yeah." Rendon sighed. "After I finished, I gave it to my station manager, but he killed it without even looking at it. As soon as I got back to the station, he wanted me right back doing the weather 'where I belonged.' Apparently he didn't want me to actually enjoy that assignment. He was just trying to teach me a lesson. So we had us a little conversation about that. It ended with me spraining my wrist, bruising his jaw, and quitting my job all in one sentence."

MacElreath smothered a laugh. "That's when you joined the fire service, I gather," she went on. She checked her notes. "You didn't join up with the Black Stand crew, it looks like. Why not?"

"Couldn't get in, for one thing," Rendon

said. "They had a full roster when I was interviewing them. I wouldn't have applied there anyway. I like the guys out there, and I respected what they were doing, but they treated me like I was their kid sister or their company mascot. Neither's a role I like to play."

MacElreath nodded, knowingly. "I see here you got on with a company up in Cloudcroft. Came in with a red card — that's impressive. Not too many women even want to be sawyers. How'd you learn to use a chain saw?"

"My mother," Rendon said, working hard to keep her tone flat, even, and professional. "She's a sculptor."

"Neat. Now, I spoke at some length with your captain out there. He speaks highly of your work. Says you've got a lock on a command of your own someday if you stay in Cloudcroft."

"That's kind of him," Rendon said. "I'd like to think I earned that."

"Tell me this, then, Amalia," pressed the chief, "if things are going so well, how come you want to leave?"

"You said you spoke to my captain, right? He told you about me?"

"That's right."

"What was the very first thing he told you about me?"

"He said you were pretty," MacElreath said.

"That's why I want to leave."

MacElreath frowned at that and nodded again. "Before we move on, I thought I'd let you know I'm hiring staff at the command level. I've got a public information officer position available if you're interested. With your news background, it might be something you're good at."

"I have no doubt I would be," Rendon said

flatly. "That's not why I'm here, though. No offense to whoever you do find for that job, but I'd rather be out there in the field making a difference with a chain saw in my hands."

"Suit yourself," the chief said, shrugging. "Okay, last couple of questions . . . Are you married?'"

"Am I married?" Rendon shot back. "I'm not sure how that's relevant."

"It's not," said Chief MacElreath, smiling. "And I like that you told me as much."

"I don't follow," said Rendon, puzzled.

"Firefighting's not widely perceived as a woman's profession, even by many women. It's mostly done by men, and a lot of men — firefighters and otherwise — have some . . . unexpected opinions about women who want in. That question I asked you wasn't pass-fail. I just wanted to see how well you could keep your cool in the face of one of those opinions. Just in case you ever come up against somebody in the field who says that sort of stuff and means it."

"But I figured you out," Rendon said.

"True," MacElreath confirmed with a nod. "That tells me something just as important. Shows you don't lose your head in a stressful situation — a job interview, in this case — and not only think fast on your feet, but you're confident in who you are. That's the sort of attitude I like in my people."

Rendon was relieved. "But, Chief, I don't even think the good ol' boys ask those types of questions anymore."

"Not anymore," MacElreath said with a wink.

Rendon thought she knew exactly what that wink meant.

"And you're right, Rendon," the chief added. "Most of those 'good ol' boys' are learning. The young boys — the rookies — they hardly know any different. Heck, I trained half of those kids myself. And if you think for one moment, I'd tolerate —" Chief MacElreath stopped. "Well, I don't have to explain it to you."

Rendon gave a knowing nod.

"All I'm saying is that everyone on this crew deserves respect," the chief began again. "We treat each other as equals. And in a few years, we truly will be an equal team — fifty-fifty — at least if I have anything to say about it. And you, Rendon, are going to be a big part of that equation."

"Me?" Rendon pointed to herself. "Does that mean you want to offer me this job?"

"Was there any doubt?" MacElreath said, as if the conclusion were too obvious to put into words. "I made that decision when I saw your résumé and called your references."

"Oh," Rendon said. It felt like a chirp coming out of her mouth. "Um . . . You didn't want to just tell me that over the phone?"

MacElreath chuckled again. "To be honest, I would have if I'd just wanted you for a sawyer. But I've got a leadership position in mind for you, and for that I needed to put you through the wringer a little."

"Leadership?" Rendon asked, grinning. "I'd love to have my own strike team, if that's what you mean."

"I wish I could," MacElreath said. "Right now I've got the budget for exactly one elite strike team — and you're on it — but the leader's already been chosen and his name is Lieutenant Jason Garret. What I can do, though, is make you a crew boss. For now. We can talk about more responsibility later, as our roster expands. Interested?"

Rendon didn't even have to think about it. "Absolutely. Although . . . let me ask you something."

"Go for it."

"What would've happened if I'd taken you up on that offer to be your public information officer?" Rendon questioned.

MacElreath blinked in surprise and laughed out loud. "Well, you would've made the person I already hired for that position very angry at you and me both. So I'm glad you didn't."

"So there was never another job?" Rendon asked, puzzled.

"There's only one place you should be," MacElreath said. "Welcome to the Firestormers."

CHAPTER THREE

Sergeant Rendon sat on a sawn log, thinking. As she did, she sharpened up the teeth of her chain saw with a long file. The old beast had been chewing up trees all day, and it was starting to go a little dull on her.

The file's back-and-forth metallic scraping made a raspy sort of music that made Rendon grin and think of her mother sitting on a stump back home doing the same thing.

"We're all cleaned up," her second sawyer, Alex, told her as he came ambling over. The cargo pockets of his fire-resistant Nomex pants bulged with the plastic wrapping from the MRE he'd eaten. His chain saw hung propped casually on one shoulder. "Are we pushing on or waiting for Raphael's crew to bump us?"

"We'll give them 'til I finish with this," Rendon replied, gesturing with her file. "Or until our ranger checks in — whichever comes first."

"Got it." Alex ambled away again to relay the news to the others.

Like the other Firestormers, Sergeant Rendon's crew was working in a bump-and-jump pattern designed to eat up miles of fire and keep the work moving smoothly. Their strike team leader back at camp — Lieutenant Jason Garrett — had established the prospective fire line on an interactive map on his laptop and divided it up into equal segments.

Sergeant Rendon's crew was slightly faster on average than the other three crews, leaving long gaps in the fire line between themselves and the other crews. Rendon hoped that Sergeant Rodgers's crew and the others could pick up the pace because gaps in the fire line weren't ideal.

Those gaps would have been fairly dangerous if not for the rangers attached to each of the crews. Unlike the sawyers and swampers working on the line, Corey Edwards and the other three rangers swept out around their crews on their own, keeping an eye on things at a safe distance.

Moving inside and outside the unfinished fire line, they monitored the progress of the fire and made reports on evolving conditions. They also stayed in contact with crew bosses, making sure the line was on course, or helping redirect it around unforeseen obstacles.

The rangers even occasionally helped direct air tankers and helicopters deployed by the Air Operations branch back at the Incident Command Post, acting like Air Force combat controllers on the ground in enemy territory. While Sergeant Rendon and her crew kept their heads down and focused on the work in front of them, Edwards and the other rangers kept them safe against the unpredictable whims of the ravenous wildfire.

A couple of minutes of filing later, Edwards's call came in on the radio.

Sergeant Rendon checked his GPS position on her datapad. That datapad was her lifeline out to Edwards and to Lieutenant Garrett at camp. It also held her maps of the area and kept her updated on the schedule of Air Operations' air tanker flyovers.

Early in her career, her first Hotshot crew had been caught unaware when an air tanker had buzzed over her line raining fire-retardant foam on the area. None of the heavy chunks had hit anyone, luckily, but spatter from the bombardment had dyed all their clothes and gear and exposed skin sickly pink for the rest of the job.

Rendon had no intention of letting that ever happen again.

"Go ahead, Edwards," Rendon said.

"Hey, Sergeant," the ranger replied. "We've, um . . . I think we have a problem."

Sergeant Rendon set her chain saw aside and stood up, her blood running cold. Edwards's GPS marker on the map showed he was about half a mile out ahead of the finished part of the line and just outside it. "What is it?"

"It's not an emergency, exactly. I mean, not for us, I guess. Well, maybe. I don't think there's even a code for it."

Sergeant Rendon frowned. Edwards didn't sound rattled or even particularly alarmed. He sounded . . . confused.

"What's going on?" she asked him.

"Well, there's . . . there's *people* out here," Edwards told her. "Right in the middle of where the next leg has to go through."

"What?" Rendon gasped. "You're kidding me, right? This area was supposed to be completely uninhabited."

"I wish I was kidding," Edwards said. "Can you come ahead and meet me? They want to talk to somebody in charge."

"Oh crud. Yeah, I'll be right there."

CHAPTER FOUR

"Where are they?" Sergeant Rendon asked her ranger, who was sitting on a rock, looking glum. She did not see anyone else.

"Okay, Edwards," she said through a wry grin, "if this is a weird ploy to get me alone in the woods, you've got some explaining to do."

The ranger looked up and flushed bright red. Two distinct shades of embarrassment shined in his eyes. His words stumbled over each other for almost thirty seconds as he hastily tried to explain that that was definitely not the case.

"Relax," Rendon told him. "I'm just teasing you. Where are these people who shouldn't be here?"

Looking somehow relieved and further embarrassed at the same time, Edwards jumped down from his rock and motioned her forward. "This way."

Sergeant Rendon set off after him through a dense cluster of black spruce and paper birch on a winding path. It looked just like every other random space between any two given trees.

"So how many people are we dealing with out here?" she asked.

"Not sure," Ranger Edwards said. "They didn't too much like me showing up unannounced. Didn't feel much like showing me around. They agreed to talk to my boss, but they wouldn't let me wait down here with them. It's probably just as well I came back, though. I don't know if you'd have been able to find the place on your own."

"I'd have you on GPS," Sergeant Rendon pointed out, gesturing with the datapad on her forearm.

"That wouldn't help much in woods like this," Ranger Edwards said, patting a tree trunk as he went by it. "Heck, if I hadn't tramped this trail down so much on my way out, I would've had a hard time finding the way back myself."

Rendon shook her head. If this nontrail was what Edwards considered easy to follow, she'd hate to have seen a difficult one.

In another few minutes of winding their way through the woods, the two of them reached their destination. The trail emptied out into a long-ago dried out streambed that split in the middle around a jagged upthrust of stones.

Beyond the stones, built onto the side of a thickly wooded hill, was the start of a tiny little village of spruce-log cabins. Wisps of smoke rose up from narrow stone chimneys and wildflowers grew up through the duff beneath the hide-curtained windows.

There were no roads, no vehicles, and no animals larger than dogs. What few dogs they could see all either immediately started barking or ran and hid in the shadows of the trees all around.

"How exactly did you find this place?" Sergeant Rendon murmured with a sidelong glance at Edwards.

"I saw the chimney smoke," he said just as quietly. "I thought a spot fire had started, so I came down here to put it out. Then I met them."

"Them" referred to the twenty or so people Edwards could see standing in front of their houses looking at the two newcomers as if they were visitors from another world.

In a way, perhaps they were.

Among the crowd was a fairly even mix of men and women and another half of the total in children. The children's faces showed a mingling of fear and curiosity, tipping toward the latter the younger the kids were. The women were all stony-eyed and quiet. The men glared with suspicion. A knot of them stood by the stones that marked the entrance to the tiny village, quietly conferring with one another. Five of them broke away from the main group and came forward as Rendon and Edwards approached.

"Well what's this now?" the one in the center said, gesturing at Rendon but looking at Edwards.

This one, the apparent leader, was older than Edwards by some twenty years and outweighed him by eighty pounds of muscle. His salt-and-pepper beard was thicker than the hair on Rendon's head. He wore a battered blue down coat with scuffed patches at the elbows, and a fur-lined leather cap covered his head. His jeans were faded sky-blue and had started to come apart slightly at the knees. A little hint of dingy off-white thermal material showed through. "You said you were bringing somebody in charge."

"Amalia Rendon," she said, stepping forward and offering a handshake. "Sergeant Amalia Rendon, if you like, of the National Elite Interagency Wildland Rapid Response Strike Force. The Firestormers."

"Never heard of you," the bearded man said, barely flicking his eyes sideways at her. He addressed his next question to Edwards. "National agency? You didn't say you were feds."

"We work for the Forest Service," Edwards stammered out. He tried to subtly back up to physically defer to Sergeant Rendon.

"What are you doing out here?" one of the other men asked.

"We'd love to know the same thing about you," Rendon said, trying to phrase that in a friendly tone. "But that can be a story for another time. Did you know you have about eleven thousand acres of fire coming your way?"

The big man frowned and looked up at the sky, which was barely visible through the thick trees. "We thought the clouds were acting a little funny. How many acres you say?"

"Eleven thousand," Rendon said. "And counting."

The big man grunted. Behind him, the others shifted their feet and frowned at each other. Rendon eventually gave up waiting for them to say something.

"I didn't catch your name," she said, looking the leader in the eyes.

"Stoyko," he said. "Peter Stoyko."

"Never heard of you," she said back with a grin. It had no effect. "Listen, Peter, we need to get you people out of here." She nodded past him at the other people watching from a distance. "Is this everyone you've got out here, or are there more spread out?"

"What do you mean get us out of here?" Stoyko grumbled. "We live here."

"Where you live will soon be a bone yard," Sergeant Rendon pointed out. "There's a hundred-foot wall of flame coming this way, and there's nothing between it and here but black spruce and birch trees."

"Where are you from?" Stoyko asked but didn't wait for a response. "Wherever it is, we do things differently here. We don't let people take what's ours. We didn't roll over for that logging company back in ninety-six, and we're not letting the federal government come in here and run us out either."

"She's trying to help you, man," Edwards piped up.

"This isn't about wanting your land, Mister Stoyko," Rendon explained. "Fifteen minutes ago we had no idea your community was even out here."

"That's how we like it," Stoyko said.

"But we've got a job to do," Rendon pressed on. "There's a fire coming, and we need to dig a line right through here to try to contain it. This streambed would make a pretty great fire break, actually, if we could clear it."

"Nope," Stoyko said.

"Nope?" Sergeant Rendon repeated. "That's it? Just nope?"

"You got jobs to do, but we got lives to live after you're done," Stoyko explained. "You want to cut some lines through these woods, but you have no idea what that's going to do to the game we live off of."

"Do you have any idea what a fire's going to do to that game?" Rendon asked.

Stoyko wasn't listening. "And now you're talking about practically digging up our front yard. I don't think so. If you've got lines to dig, go dig them someplace else, thank you."

Stoyko didn't flinch as he said that last bit, but the men behind him didn't uniformly share his conviction. The other one who'd spoken did so again now, though he avoided any eye contact with Sergeant Rendon.

"I don't know, Pete," he mumbled. "If the fire's as bad as they say . . ."

"They're some kind of firemen, right?" Stoyko replied. He looked at Edwards first and then turned and smiled at Sergeant Rendon. "You're fire*men*?"

"Firefighters," Sergeant Rendon said.

"So go fight it, then," Stoyko said. "We're law-abiding citizens who own property. It's your job to keep that fire away from us, right? So go do it. Get it done. Just leave us out of it."

"What if they can't?" the other man said.

"They're with a federal agency, Mike," Stoyko shot back. "They've obviously got plenty of money. Look at that gizmo on her arm. Look at those fancy glasses and watch the kid's wearing. Listen to those airplanes flying over all day. They can handle it."

Ranger Edwards backed up a step and touched the temple of his safety goggles. Built onto them was a small fiber-optic camera and projector that connected wirelessly to the smart watch on his wrist. Together, they performed much the same function as Rendon's datapad.

"Maybe, they can," Mike said. "But shouldn't we be sure?" He looked at Sergeant Rendon for the first time, then back at Stoyko. "Maybe there's somebody she can call to confirm all this for us. Like her boss or something. I don't know."

"So you won't take my word for it even though I've been staring this fire in the face all day," Rendon asked, "but you'll take it from my boss over the radio?"

"Sounds reasonable to me, Pete," Mike said. The other men mumbled their agreement. "Just to be sure, you know."

"Guys, I'm telling you —"

Sergeant Rendon stopped at a tentative touch on her shoulder from Edwards.

"We're going to have to call Lieutenant Garrett about all this anyway," Edwards pointed out. "We don't have a whole lot of time. Maybe they'll listen to him. Or if not him, then maybe Chief MacElreath."

Sergeant Rendon closed her eyes for a second and took a deep breath. When she opened her eyes again, she had regained composure. She nodded at Edwards and turned back to Stoyko.

"I do have to call in about this," she said. "Whether I end up having to move the lines or whatever, this information's got to work its way back up to Incident Command. But to give them the full picture, I need to look around. I need to know how many people you have here, how spread out you all are, that sort of thing. I have to make a full report. The sooner I can get that done, the sooner we're out of your hair."

Stoyko narrowed his eyes at her and crossed his arms.

"Also, we're a little hungry," she added.

The MRE she'd eaten wasn't as filling after a morning of hard work as it might have been.

Stoyko sighed and turned his back on Rendon and Edwards, trudging back toward the village. The other men turned around to go with him.

"Fine," he grumped over his shoulder. "Come on, then. Just make that call soon."

CHAPTER FIVE

Stoyko didn't stay with them long. He took them to a modest cabin in the center of the small village and dropped them off with a hard-eyed woman in her twenties named Natalya. He told her to show the two of them around, answer their questions, and then come get him. Before she could protest, he stomped off to go huddle in conversation with the other men once more.

Natalya didn't care for Rendon's presence, if the scowl on her face was any indication, but she took an instant liking to Edwards.

When the ranger admitted he hadn't eaten lunch, Natalya disappeared into the cabin and returned with a plate stacked with wedges of flat bread, nuts, and dried fruits. Edwards tucked into it as the tour began, earning himself a disappointed glare when he offered some to Rendon.

The tour didn't actually take very long. There were a dozen cabins spread out in a loose cluster along what had once been the streambed. They were all in decent condition and had been built by hand within just the last couple of decades.

Nowhere in evidence were there signs of any modern conveniences, such as plumbing or electricity, even from gas-powered generators. Sergeant Rendon didn't see so much as a mountain bike for getting around. The most modern quality anyone showed out here was their clothes and the way they talked. Natalya also made it a point to be sure Rendon knew the bows and rifles the men used to hunt game were the best and newest their money could buy.

What Natalya refused to speak about was why these people were out here in the first place. They survived on hunting, fishing, and growing meager crops in a sheltered garden. Every once in a blue moon, they trekked to the nearest town — miles and miles away — to trade. They rarely brought back anything other than clothes, hand tools, or the supplies they needed to make ammunition for hunting.

As for what, if anything specific, drove them to live so far out here on their own, Natalya remained tight-lipped.

When the tour was over, Natalya told the visitors to wait while she went to find Peter again. Edwards had just finished his bread.

"I'm not sure what to do right now, Edwards," Rendon muttered when the locals were out of earshot. "These nuts act like they want to get themselves burned up."

"They're not nuts just because they want to live out here by themselves," Edwards replied, looking down at his shoes. "Maybe they're just big fans of Emerson or something."

Rendon murmured, skeptically, "'Simplify, simplify, simplify.' That sort of thing?"

"Yeah," Edwards said. "Except, Thoreau said that. Not Emerson."

"That's all well and good," Rendon told him, "but I don't understand why they're digging their heels in when we're here trying to help them."

"We work for the government," Edwards said, shrugging as if that answered everything.

"Right," Rendon said, as if that was her point.

"Well, not everybody's been treated fairly by the government. Some people like to kick up a fuss about that. Others just look for someplace they can live and let live and not be bothered." He shrugged.

"Hm," Rendon murmured. Her ranger had a point. Edwards had a point, and he knew the difference between Emerson and Thoreau. "You and me should talk more often."

Edwards looked away with a blush and scratched the back of his neck. Rendon couldn't help but notice the dopey grin he tried to hide.

Stoyko came back with some of his cronies in tow. Natalya followed a few paces back. "You ready to make that call yet?" the big man asked.

"Just doing that now," Rendon told him, gesturing with her radio. "Give me a second."

She stepped away and opened a radio link to Garrett back at camp. "Lieutenant, it's Rendon. We've got a problem."

"Yeah, my tablet shows that you and Edwards are off the line," Lieutenant Garrett replied. "What's going on?"

Rendon filled him in as quickly as she could.

"Oh crud," Lieutenant Garrett said when she was finished.

"That's what I said."

"And they don't want to leave?" Garrett asked.

"They're definitely not going to leave just because I told them to."

"So how do you want to play it?" asked the lieutenant. "I can tear them a new one for not listening to you, if you like, but I'm hesitant to just say what I know you've already been telling them. You're their point of contact with us, whether they like it or not. I don't want to undermine your authority with them."

Rendon smiled appreciatively. Lieutenant Garrett was young and hadn't had more than an academic understanding of wildland firefighting before joining the Firestormers. Yes, his appointment as strike team leader had been purely political, but he was a sharp guy.

"I've got an idea," she said. She quickly laid out his part in it and told him what she intended to do after that.

"All right," Garrett said, somewhat dubiously. "Let's hope your acting chops are up to snuff." The lieutenant chuckled.

"You got it, Lieutenant," Rendon said, after a moment.

Sergeant Rendon broke the connection and walked back over to where Stoyko and the others could hear her.

"Sorry about that," she said. "Federal bureaucracy. You know how it is. You can't go ten feet without jumping through just as many hoops."

A couple of the locals nodded knowingly.

"Anyway, they should be able to put me through to the commander in charge of this area," Sergeant Rendon went on. She keyed her radio, said her name, and uttered a string of official-sounding gibberish like she was a soldier in a movie on a classified mission. She finished with, "Come in, command."

"Garrett," the lieutenant said, his voice filled with weary boredom. "What is it now, Rendon?"

"Sir, I have the leader of that local community here with me. I thought maybe you could talk to him."

"Give him the radio," Lieutenant Garrett said.

"Yes, sir." Rendon obliged.

She passed Stoyko her radio and gave Edwards a flat, even look in response to his expression of complete bafflement.

"Who is this?" Lieutenant Garrett asked. "What's your name?

"Sir, my name's Peter Stoyko," the big man replied. "I'm speaking on behalf of my friends and family out here."

"Great," Garrett said. "You guys aren't a bunch of criminals hiding from the law, are you?"

"No, sir," Stoyko said, blinking in surprise.

"Are you terrorists, running some kind of training camp?"

"I don't even know what that means."

"You're not illegals, are you, hiding out from immigration?"

"No, sir," Stoyko told him. That suggestion, over the others, seemed to offend him.

"Then I don't care what you do," Lieutenant Garrett said. "It's a free country. Now give the radio back to my firefighters."

Frowning and confused, Stoyko looked at the radio a moment then tried to hand it over to Edwards. Edwards, who looked just as confused as Stoyko did, handed the radio back to Rendon.

"Rendon?" Lieutenant Garrett's voice barked over the speaker.

"Sir?" she asked.

"Quit wasting time. Get back to your crew and get your line done."

"What about these people?" Rendon asked.

"Your problem, not mine. Garrett out."

Lieutenant Garrett broke the connection. Rendon just stared at her radio with blank eyes. When she looked up, Stoyko and the other locals were frowning at her — specifically, at her radio — with troubled expressions.

A few seconds later, her datapad vibrated silently as a text message came in. She glanced at it. "That felt horrible," it read. "Please don't ever ask me to do that again." Sergeant Rendon smothered the urge to grin.

"Well, that wasn't worth much," Stoyko mumbled.

"It's like he didn't even care we're here," the man named Mike added.

"He cares," Edwards said, instinctively coming to his lieutenant's defense. Rendon shot him a look. "He's supposed to, anyway."

"Listen," Rendon said, making herself the voice of reason. "He's behind a desk, shuffling papers and watching things on a computer screen. He doesn't know the situation out here. He doesn't know what you're up against. And honestly, I don't think you do either. Not really. But if you let me, I can show you."

"How?" Mike asked.

"I'm going to take you out to the fire front," Rendon said. "Once you see it for yourselves, you can decide for yourselves what you want to do."

Edwards's eyes turned as wide as saucers, his face paling with shock. "No way Lieutenant Garrett's okay with that," he muttered.

A frown of legitimate frustration darkened Rendon's face. "Garrett made this my problem. This is my solution."

The locals looked back and forth from Edwards to Rendon then turned inward to have a quick conference on the subject. When it broke up, Stoyko stepped forward.

"Tell you what," he began. "We'll let you take us out to see your fire, just so as you can say you did it. It's not going to change anything, though."

"We'll see," Rendon told him. To Edwards, she said, "I need a high vantage inside the fire line. Somewhere with a wide view. Find me one."

Edwards hesitated, cringing under the hard look Rendon was giving him. Fortunately, when he was confused or out of his element, he defaulted to obedience. Holding up his smart watch, he engaged his local area map and scanned through it using the tiny projector built into his goggles.

As Edwards looked for a suitable spot, Peter Stoyko turned to face Natalya, who'd watched the proceedings with avid interest. He made a vague shooing motion toward her, gesturing for her to go back to where the rest of the community looked on.

"We're going to go take a look at this fire of theirs," he told her. "We'll be back soon. Go tell the rest of them."

Natalya nodded once and dashed over to where the women — and all the rest of the men — waited. She spoke to them rapidly in low tones.

"Got a spot," Edwards said.

Sergeant Rendon came over to him, and he swiped a file from his smart watch to the datapad on her forearm. He spoke as Rendon opened her own map and centered it on the location he'd chosen. "It's about two hundred yards inside the fire line. There's a path up the side of this ridge. I used it to spot for an air tanker run when the crew behind us first bumped us out here. The computer models say we should have plenty of time to get up there, look around, and get back before the fire gets there."

The sophisticated fire-modeling computer program Behave could predict how a wildfire was likely to grow and spread. Incident Command used it to decide how to deploy its strike teams. But the rangers in the field were essential for sending back firsthand data to refine the program's information.

"Looks good," Rendon said. "How long out there?"

"It's about twenty minutes away, if we hurry. I hope these guys are good hikers."

"We ready here?" Peter Stoyko said, coming over to where they were waiting. The four men who made up his little cadre followed him.

Before Rendon could answer, Natalya strolled up beside Stoyko.

"What do you think you're doing?" he asked her.

"I'm going to see the fire," Natalya said, staring up at him defiantly.

"Stay here," he told her. "This could be dangerous."

"I'm going," Natalya replied matter-of-factly.

"We can get six people there as easy as five," Sergeant Rendon said. "As long as we don't waste any more time. Let's go."

With a nudge, she got Ranger Edwards moving and followed him. Natalya fell in right behind them without another word.

Stoyko heaved a sigh and got moving as well, but not before turning to the man next to him and muttering, "Never have kids."

"Don't look at me, bud," the man said. "I warned you."

CHAPTER SIX

As Sergeant Rendon trekked toward the fire overlook, she hoped without hope that Stoyko and his community would come to their senses.

The trek wasn't long as the crow flies, but the thick ground cover and the uneven terrain made it take twice as long as it should have. As the land carried them up higher, the breaks in the trees grew wider, allowing them to see more smoke darkening the skies from the near distance. The roar of the fire came to them as a background whisper that steadily rose in volume. Off to one side, they could hear the faint whine of chain saws where Rendon's crew was still working on the fire line. They left that comforting noise behind and tucked in toward the ever-spreading fire front.

Edwards slowed his ground-eating stride for a bit, falling back to walk beside Rendon. The pair of them were in the lead with the locals strung out behind them in a line. He tugged nervously at the cuffs of his Nomex work shirt, working himself up to say something.

"What is it, Edwards?" Sergeant Rendon asked him, keeping her voice low.

"Just wanted to tell you," he began, looking everywhere but at her. "Just wanted you to know I'm sorry about back there. What I said."

"About what?"

"About Lieutenant Garrett not being okay with this," Edwards continued. "I saw you talking to him by yourself. I should have figured you were up to something. I didn't mean to undermine you. I hope I didn't mess things up."

"You're fine," Sergeant Rendon told him, trying not to laugh in the face of his uncomfortable sincerity. "I got these guys right where I want 'em. We're nearly there, right?"

Ranger Edwards checked his watch. "Yeah, it's just up here." He glanced up into the projection field on his goggles. "Fire's coming on fast. We'd better hustle."

The ranger jogged back up into the lead, and Rendon looked back over her shoulder to relay Edwards's update to the others. They tightened up their line just in time to huff and haul themselves up the tricky goat path that led up the last ridge to the vantage Edwards had chosen.

One by one, they came around a boulder at the top, held in place by the roots of an old tree onto an overlook with a sheer drop on the other side. There they beheld the immensity of the fire spread out across the foothills.

"Holy cow . . .," Natalya gasped.

CHAPTER SEVEN

Below them, the landscape resembled a war zone. A fleet of planes and helicopters buzzed back and forth over the area, all under the coordination of the Air Operations branch back at Incident Command. The planes — enormous air tankers — swooped low over the ground releasing ten-thousand-gallon payloads of fire-retardant chemicals. The choppers were even more precise, dropping smaller payloads on specific targets from internal tanks and from collapsible two-thousand-gallon buckets.

The sky above the aircraft fire retardants belonged to a smaller unit of just a handful of planes and helicopters. These were the spotters and the search-and-rescue craft that acted as Incident Command's eyes in the sky.

As impressive as the air show was, however, it paled in comparison to what was happening on the ground. The fire had come closer to the ridge than Edwards had predicted, affording the onlookers a better-than-expected view of it. Searing orange fingers clawed their way across exposed overgrowth as if to drag the fire bodily behind them. The heat from them was so intense that even the ground that wasn't actively burning steamed and smoldered toward the ignition point. The land seemed to be boiling away from within.

Where trees stood outside the fire front, the scene was even more dire. As thin, sinister tendrils of the fire crept or raced along the ground between them, the trees seemed to shudder in terror. Hot embers carried on the wind tore bright orange holes in their canopies right before the witnesses' eyes. Smoke began to rise on the side of the bark closest to the fire. Sap in the trees' veins bubbled and expanded like water in a kettle on the stove. All across the fire line, Rendon could see spots where escaping sap bubbled and ran down the trees' skin like wounds. And that was only where that boiling sap could find some way to escape the tree.

Where it couldn't . . .

"Look right down there," Rendon said, pointing at a knot of pines just ahead of the fire front at the base of a hill. All of the trees there were smoking, but on none of them could she see sap running. That meant the pressure inside at least some of them was building . . . building . . . building . . .

With a thunderclap that made Edwards jump, one of the trees in the center exploded as the trapped, boiling sap tore it apart from the inside. Before any of the locals could say anything, another blew. The fire was in among the trees on the ground now, and in just a matter of seconds, it took hold of them. Winding up the trunks, the flame torched up all the way into the canopy, turning the ruined knot of seventy-foot trees into a towering wall of hundred-foot-tall flames.

"Good lord," Peter Stoyko whispered.

The look of horror on his face said it all. The knot of trees the explosions had come from represented in miniature the magnitude of the rest of the blaze they were staring at. The interior was completely lost in a mountain of black smoke turning to thick gray as it pierced the sky. The true center closest to the ignition point was impossible to see, but the expanding outer core was a nightmare of living flames.

They gnawed on the remaining tree trunks and greedily flowed outward to fill any space along the topography that their initial mad rush had left unburned. In places where the trunks, the understory, and the canopy of the forest were fully involved, the flames roared like on the surface of the sun.

The fire played havoc with the weather as well. As it created unimaginable heat, the air it heated shot skyward carrying the smoke and creating convection currents. The cooler air around the fire was sucked in to replace the rising hot air, giving birth to constant winds that blew in around the fire. The tallest of the blazes danced in the winds like monsters.

"Look," Rendon said, pointing into a different section, closer to the heart of the fire. She practically had to shout to be heard over the roar of wind and flame. "That's what we're up against down there. Watch."

Before the locals' horrified eyes, the wind whipped and warped the flames on an isolated stand of spruce into a tornado of fire.

The twister danced through the trees, sealing their doom as it caught them all ablaze one by one. Two of them exploded into burning chunks in the thirty seconds the terrifying scene took before billowing smoke covered it.

"You're fighting that?" Natalya asked, her eyes wide, almost to the point of being in shock.

"Yeah," Sergeant Rendon told her, told them all. "My team's back there right now digging out a defensive barrier with a bunch of chain saws and hand tools."

"You can't put that out," Peter Stoyko said, his eyes as wide as his daughter's.

"We're not here to put it out," Rendon explained. "We're just trying to stop it so it doesn't eat up this whole place. What you've got to ask yourself now, is what happens if we can't. Your homes are right where our fire lines need to go to contain this. We can adjust inward a little, but you know this forest better than we do. What if it's harder to move through than we expect? One shift in this wind can push that fire up on us fast. If we're digging out in front of your houses, do you really still want to be in them if we have to fall back and abandon the area?"

"No," Stoyko said. His voice was so soft his words were nearly lost. "We've seen enough. We should get back. We need to get ready to leave."

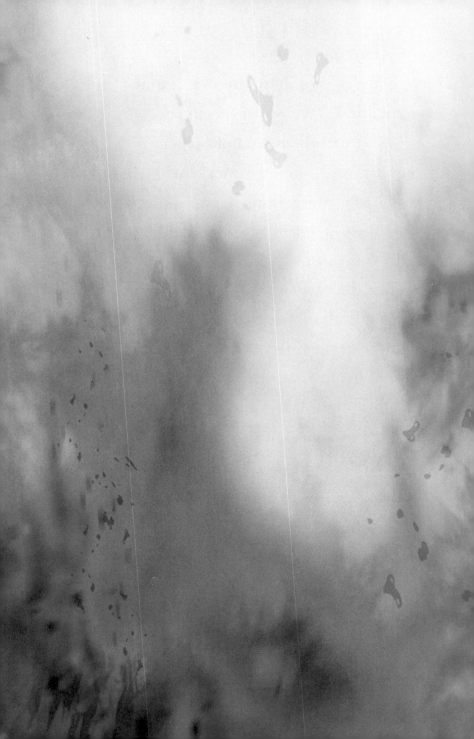

CHAPTER EIGHT

The scene that greeted them when they got back to Stoyko's village was a surprise to all the local men, though not to Natalya. Edwards looked just as shocked as the men did. Rendon less so.

Everyone still in the village was waiting by the stones that split the streambed, dressed for a hike and carrying knapsacks bulging with supplies. They were as laden with gear and provisions as the Firestormers had been when they'd first hiked out to the line. Even the children not small enough to need to be carried themselves were lugging small patched-up sacks.

"What's this now?" Stoyko said, taking the scene in. He looked at Natalya.

"I told them you said we needed to be ready to go by the time you got back," Natalya said, daring him with her eyes to reprimand her for it. "Momma took care of it."

"You're in big trouble, young lady," he grumbled at her. She grinned.

"All right, everyone," Rendon said, stepping up to address the crowd. "You've got a long way to go." She gestured to her ranger, standing behind her. "This is Corey Edwards. I'm going to need you to follow him and do your level best to keep up. You've got a long way to go and not much time to get there. Edwards will be leading the line making sure no one gets lost."

"Sounds fine to me," Edwards said,

stepping up beside her but speaking quietly just to her. "But where am I taking them?"

"Camp first," Rendon said. "Let them rest, get them fed, then take them back to where we parked the buggies. Lieutenant Garrett's got some Red Cross volunteers on the way there to pick them up."

"Already?"

"Of course," Rendon said with a wink. "What do you think I was talking to him about for so long before I made him pretend to be a jerk in front of everybody?"

Edwards grinned. "You're lucky Mister Stoyko over there isn't as stubborn as I thought he was."

"Nobody's so stubborn he'll put his whole community at risk just so he doesn't have to take orders from me," Rendon said.

"Speaking of . . ."

As the villagers began to gather around,

Peter Stoyko came up to Rendon with Natalya in tow. He looked down at Rendon with blank, hooded eyes. Rendon nodded for Edwards to go ahead and get people ready to move. He did so.

"Where are we headed?" Stoyko asked.

Rendon told him the plan.

"Hm. Your lieutenant's not going to be too happy to see us all."

"I'll handle him," Rendon said. "He's much nicer in person than on the radio."

"What happens once we're out of the way?"

"We're still sorting that out," Rendon admitted, "but we've got the Red Cross on it. They'll be able to get you someplace comfortable pretty quickly. They'll be able to let you know how soon you can get back to your homes."

"If we can," Stoyko said.

Rendon frowned. "That's fair. You've seen what we're up against. I can't make you any promises — this business is too unpredictable for that — but let me tell you this . . . We're going to do everything we can to keep this fire from getting anywhere near your homes. This is our top priority now. We're going to do everything we can for you. If there's anybody out here working this fire who can save your village, it's us."

"I hope you're right," Stoyko replied glumly. "We'll see." He turned away, paused, then turned back once more. "Hey, what'd you say your name was?"

"Amalia. Amalia Rendon. Sergeant Amalia Rendon, if you like."

"You're all right, Sergeant," Stoyko told her. "For a fed, anyways."

"You too, Peter," Rendon said. "For a bull-headed mountain man."

Stoyko grunted and gave her the barest hint of a smile before turning away with his daughter and joining the others forming up around Edwards. As the long procession out of the village began, Rendon keyed Lieutenant Garrett on the radio.

"Lieutenant, this is Rendon," she said.

"I read you," he replied. "Did it work?"

"It worked. They're on the move," Rendon responded. "I'm heading back to the fire line to help out my crew."

"Good work, Sergeant," said Garrett. "Hope to see you soon."

Rendon snorted a little laugh. "From the looks of this thing, sir, I wouldn't count on that."

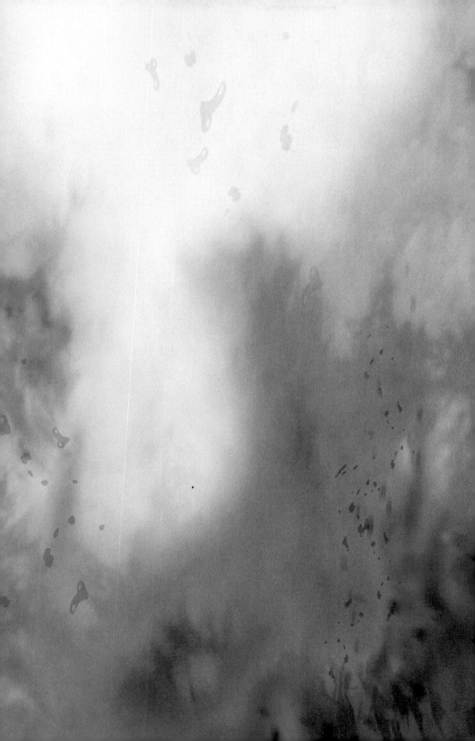

ABOUT THE AUTHOR

Carl Bowen is a father, husband, and writer living in Lawrenceville, Georgia. He has published a handful of novels, short stories, and comics. For Stone Arch Books and Capstone, Carl has retold *20,000 Leagues Under the Sea* (by Jules Verne), *The Strange Case of Dr. Jekyll and Mr. Hyde* (by Robert Louis Stevenson), *The Jungle Book* (by Rudyard Kipling), "Aladdin and His Wonderful Lamp" (from *A Thousand and One Nights*), *Julius Caesar* (by William Shakespeare), and *The Murders in the Rue Morgue* (by Edgar Allan Poe). Carl's novel, *Shadow Squadron: Elite Infantry*, earned a starred review from *Kirkus Book Reviews*.

GLOSSARY

bureaucracy (byur-AHK-ruh-see) — strict and complicated regulations, often blamed for slow or illogical government action

civilization (si-vuh-luh-ZAY-shuhn) — a highly developed and organized society

Global Positioning System (GLOH-buhl puh-ZI-shuh-ning SISS-tuhm) — an electronic tool used to find the location of an object; this system is often called GPS

inferno (in-FUR-noh) — a very large and dangerous fire

permafrost (PUR-muh FROST) — a layer of frozen earth underground that never thaws, even in summer

thermal (THUR-muhl) — something that is designed to hold in body heat

FIREFIGHTING EQUIPMENT

PULASKI AXE
A single-bit ax with an adze-shaped hoe extending from the back.

MCLEOD
A combination hoe and rake used especially by the U.S. Forest Service in firefighting.

CHAIN SAW
A tool that cuts wood with a circular chain that is driven by a motor and made up of many connected sharp metal teeth. Sawyers use chain saws to fell trees on the fire line.

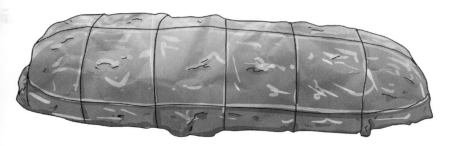

FIRE SHELTER
A small, aluminized tent offering protection in an emergency. The shelter reflects radiant heat and provides breathable air if a firefighter becomes trapped within a blaze.

DRIPTORCH
A handheld canister containing flammable fuel. When ignited, firefighters use driptorches to "drip" flames onto the ground for a controlled burn.

TWO-WAY RADIO
A small radio for receiving and sending messages.

WILDFIRE FACTS

Nearly 90% of wildfires are started by humans. Most of these fires begin by accidental causes, including careless campfires and poorly discarded cigarettes.

Lightning is the leading cause of natural wildfires. Every day, lightning strikes the Earth more than 100,000 times, and 10–20% of those strikes ignite a fire. However, most lightning fires are small and burn out quickly.

An average of 1.2 million acres of forest burns in the United States every year. In 2015, more than 10 million acres burned, setting a new record. Battling these fires costs $1.7 billion.

In extreme wildfires, flames can tower more than 165 feet in the air and reach temperatures of 2,200 degrees Fahrenheit.

The Great Miramichi Fire is the largest wildfire ever recorded. The blaze burned more than 3 million acres throughout New Brunswick, Canada, and Maine, in October 1825. During the fire, 160 lives were lost.

On June 30, 2013, nineteen members of the Granite City Hotshots were killed during the Yarnell Hill Fire in Yarnell, Arizona. It was the deadliest day for U.S. firefighters since the terrorist attacks on September 11, 2001.

READ MORE . . .

FIRESTORMERS

FIRESTORMERS
FIRE FRONT
BY CARL BOWEN

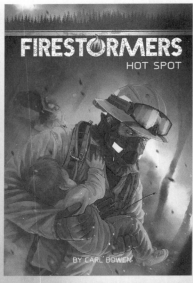

FIRESTORMERS
HOT SPOT
BY CARL BOWEN

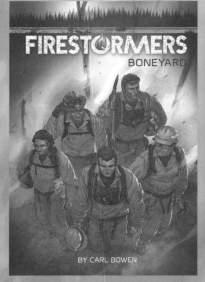

FIRESTORMERS
BONEYARD
BY CARL BOWEN

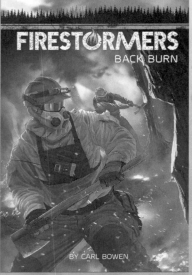

FIRESTORMERS
BACK BURN
BY CARL BOWEN

THEN CHECK OUT . . .

SHADOW SQUADRON

ALSO BY CARL BOWEN

ONLY FROM STONE ARCH BOOKS

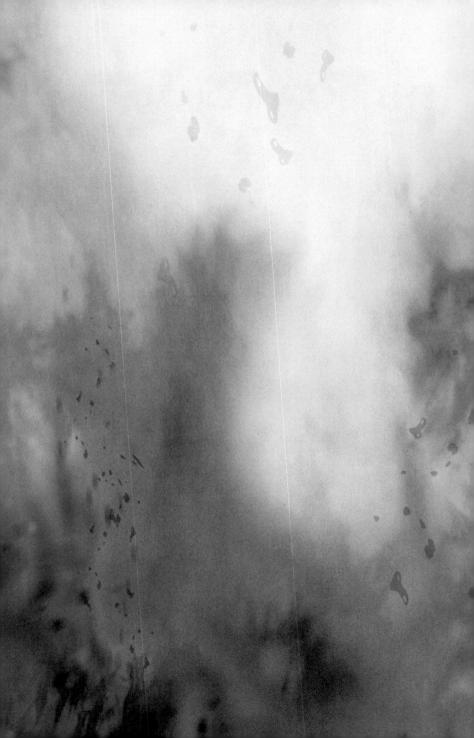